Lost in
NYC
A SUBWAY ADVENTURE

LITTLE MAVERICK GRAPHIC NOVEL READING LIST
EMPIRE STATE CENTER FOR THE BOOK GREAT READS
CONNECTICUT NUTMEG AWARD NOMINEE
ALSC GRAPHIC NOVELS READING LIST
KIRKUS PRIZE NOMINEE
SCHOOL LIBRARY JOURNAL BEST BOOKS
ABC BEST BOOKS FOR YOUNG READERS LIST
A JUNIOR LIBRARY GUILD SELECTION

For my father, whose answers to my questions made
the whole subway car fall silent to listen.   *–Nadja*

For all those who live without fear of getting lost.
And for our children, the real Pablo and Alicia,
who will soon find their way.   *–Sergio & Lola*

Editorial Director & Book Design: FRANÇOISE MOULY

Colors: LOLA MORAL

SERGIO GARCÍA SÁNCHEZ'S artwork was drawn in orange pencil
and ballpoint pen and then colored digitally by Lola Moral.

FOR VISUAL READERS
TOON
GRAPHICS

A TOON Graphic™ © 2015 Nadja Spiegelman, Sergio García Sánchez & TOON Books, an imprint of RAW Junior, LLC, 27 Greene Street, New York, NY 10013. Subway Map © Metropolitan Transportation Authority, used by permission. No part of this book may be used or reproduced in any manner whatsoever without written permission except in the case of brief quotations embodied in critical articles and reviews. TOON Graphics™, TOON Books®, LITTLE LIT® and TOON Into Reading!™ are trademarks of RAW Junior, LLC. All rights reserved.   Library of Congress Cataloging-in-Publication Data: Spiegelman, Nadja.   Lost in NYC : a subway adventure/ by Nadja Spiegelman & Sergio García Sánchez.   pages cm.--   Summary: "After getting separated from his teacher, his classmates, and his trip partner during an outing to the Empire State Building, Pablo, the new kid in school, learns to navigate the New York City subway system as well as his own feelings towards making new friends and living in a big city"–Provided by publisher. ISBN 978-1-935179-81-8   1. Graphic novels. [1. Graphic novels. 2. Subways–Fiction. 3. School field trips–Fiction. 4. Friendship–Fiction. 5. Moving, Household–Fiction. 6. New York (N.Y.)–Fiction.] I. García Sánchez, Sergio, 1967- II. Title.   PZ7.7.S65Lo 2015   741.5'973--dc23   2014028852 All our books are Smyth Sewn (the highest library-quality binding available) and printed with soy-based inks on acid-free, woodfree paper harvested from responsible sources. Printed in China by C&C Offset Printing Co., Ltd. Distributed to the trade by Consortium Book Sales & Distribution, a division of Ingram Content Group; orders (866) 400-5351; ips@ingramcontent.com; www.cbsd.com. A Spanish edition, *Perdidos en NYC: Una Aventura en el Metro* is also available.

ISBN 978-1-935179-81-8 (hardcover English edition)
ISBN 978-1-943145-48-5 (softcover English edition)
ISBN 978-1-935179-85-6 (hardcover Spanish edition)
ISBN 978-1-943145-42-3 (softcover Spanish edition)
19 20 21 22 23 24   C&C 15 14 13 12 11 10 9 8 7 6 5
www.TOON-BOOKS.com

MTA OFFICIALLY LICENSED

THE *EMPIRE STATE BULDING* WAS BUILT IN *1931*.

AT THAT TIME, IT WAS THE *TALLEST* BUILDING IN THE WORLD. IT'S IN MIDTOWN, WHERE MANHATTAN'S BEDROCK IS CLOSE TO THE SURFACE. IT'S GOOD TO ANCHOR SKYSCRAPERS IN BEDROCK WHEN YOU WANT THEM TO GROW TALL.

BUT, THIRTY YEARS EARLIER, WHEN MANHATTAN BEGAN CONSTRUCTION ON ITS UNDERGROUND SUBWAY SYSTEM, THE BEDROCK WAS A PROBLEM. BECAUSE OF THE ROCK, AND BECAUSE MANY BUILDINGS HAD ALREADY BEEN BUILT, TUNNELS COULDN'T GO VERY DEEP UNDER THE SURFACE. SO, CONSTRUCTION WORKERS USED A METHOD KNOWN AS CUT-AND-COVER

THEY OPENED STREETS LIKE BROADWAY AND DUG A TRENCH CLOSE TO THE SURFACE.

NEW JERSEY

MANHATTAN

BROOKLYN

THE BRONX

CENTRAL PARK

QUEENS

WHEN ENGINEERS HAD TO LINK THE ISLAND OF MANHATTAN TO THE BRONX AND BROOKLYN, THEY CAME UP WITH UNDERWATER TUNNELS. CAST-IRON TUBES WERE PLACED UNDERNEATH THE HARLEM RIVER AND THE EAST RIVER

THAT'S WHY MANY PLATFORMS AND TRACKS IN THE NEW YORK SUBWAY GET SOME DAYLIGHT—AND SOMETIMES EVEN RAIN...

IN OTHER PLACES IN THE CITY, ENGINEERS HAD TO DIG *VERY DEEP*. AT THE 42ND ST. STATION, FOR EXAMPLE, FIVE SUBWAY TRACKS HAD TO PASS THROUGH THE SAME AREA. THEY DUG THIRTY-FIVE FEET INTO THE GROUND. THAT'S ALMOST THE HEIGHT OF A FOUR-STORY BUILDING!

SO, WHERE ARE YOU FROM?

NOWHERE. MY DAD HAS TO MOVE A LOT FOR HIS JOB.

WHEN THE SUBWAY OPENED IN 1904, IT WAS THE *FASTEST* IN THE WORLD.

NEW YORK WAS THE FIRST CITY TO CONSTRUCT A **FOUR-TRACK** SUBWAY SYSTEM. FOUR TRACKS ALLOW EXPRESS TRAINS AND LOCAL TRAINS TO RUN SEPARATELY.

23

25

33

ABOUT THE AUTHORS

NADJA SPIEGELMAN is the Eisner Award-nominated author of the Zig and Wikki series of science comics for young children. She is a native New Yorker, who prides herself on important subway know-how, such as where to stand to get a seat, and how to sleep without missing her stop. She began taking the subway alone when she was eleven years old. Her favorite train is the Q train because it goes on a bridge over the East River, and the view of the Manhattan skyline is beautiful every time.

One of the many preparatory sketches made by the artist.

SERGIO GARCÍA SÁNCHEZ, a professor of comics in Angoulême, France and at the University of Granada, Spain, is one of Europe's most celebrated experimental cartoonists. His work has been published in over forty-five books and translated into nine languages. He lives in Granada with his wife and collaborator, Lola Moral, who colored the art for this book and provided the translation for the Spanish edition, *Perdidos en NYC: Una Aventura en el Metro*. They have two children, Pablo and Alicia.

BEHIND THE SCENES: SERGIO AND THE COP

This is Sergio's first book published in the U.S. and is based on his first trip to New York City. He filled notebook after notebook with sketches and rode the subway for days. When he went into the 96th Street subway station, he began photographing all the details he knew he would need: the vending machines, the turnstiles, and the signs. At some point, he realized that he had attracted the attention of a cop, so he hurried down the stairs. Once on the platform, he started taking pictures again. Turning around, he spotted someone in his view screen…the cop who had been following him! Fortunately, a train was entering the station at that moment. As soon as the doors opened, Sergio jumped in, eager to escape the unwanted attention. To celebrate his own adventure, Sergio decided to show himself and the cop in virtually every spread of this book. Hop on a subway with them and enjoy the behind-the-scenes adventure!

THE BEGINNINGS OF THE SUBWAY

By the late 1800s, when talk of a subway system began, public transit in New York City was already thriving. There were trains, ferries, and many horse-drawn carriages. What it lacked, however, was unification and efficiency. The roads in New York City were largely unpaved and plagued by street congestion. Transportation had to move off the street. The first attempt was in 1867, when a self-trained engineer named Charles T. Harvey built the first elevated train line, nicknamed the "one-legged railroad" because it ran on a single track! Service on the line was initially provided by cable cars, but they were replaced four years later by steam locomotives.

Charles T. Harvey making a test run, December 7, 1867.

The now-abandoned City Hall station, which was the focus of the 1904 subway opening ceremonies.

Even though elevated train lines were becoming quite prevalent in the city, interest grew for developing an underground rapid transit railroad, partly in competition with other cities and partly to help develop outlying areas. Construction of these early subways was grueling. Building crews had to excavate the subway lines by hand. This was slow, difficult, and dangerous work. The New York City subway tunnels required close to eight thousand laborers. Thousands were injured during construction, and some died.

Rock work at the entrance to the East River Tunnel.

The first underground line was opened on October 27, 1904, almost thirty-five years after the first elevated line (and in the same part of town)! When the system opened for business, more than one hundred thousand people stood in line to take a ride on the first subway train. The new system featured many innovations, including the use of electric power, which helped reduce the city's air pollution. Also unique was the four-track design that could run at both local and express speeds. At the time, it was the fastest public transportation system in the world. Hence the slogan: "City Hall to Harlem in 15 minutes!"

H. M. Pettit, Illustrations from January 31, 1903, Harpers Weekly.

A 1903 illustration of the proposed subway station at Columbus Circle, showing architectural details.

Arthur Weindorf, Architectural Rendering, 1935, Avery Architecture and Fine Arts Library.

A 1935 cross-section view of the underground and elevated transportation network at 34th Street and 6th Avenue (Herald Square). The building on the left is Macy's Department Store.

COMPETING TRANSIT COMPANIES

In the beginning, the subway system was built by two separate private companies, the IRT (Interborough Rapid Transit) and the BMT (Brooklyn-Manhattan Transit). This created two different networks of trains, which did not connect to each other. The IRT and the BMT were hit hard during the Great Depression in the 1930s. On June 1, 1940, the city took over the companies and began a slow unification of the system. It closed many of the elevated lines and created new transfer tunnels to connect the two networks.

Although now unified into a single network, there are still traces of the competing companies in the subway today. The numbered train lines were part of the IRT system. The J, L, M, N, Q, R, and Z were part of the BMT. The A, B, C, D, E, F, and G were part of a third company run by the city's Board of Transportation itself, called the IND (Independent Subway System). The trains on the letter lines (BMT/IND) are longer and wider than those on the number lines (IRT). Therefore, an A train cannot fit into a 6 train tunnel.

Brand new station at Euclid Avenue on the IND Fulton Street Line (A, C), just before service began running on the line, November 23, 1948.

"Euclid Avenue," November 23, 1948, Collection of: Frank Pfuhler.

WHY ARE THERE NO H, I, K, O, P, T, U, V, W, X, OR Y TRAINS?

The H, K, T, V, and W trains did once exist, but they have since been closed or combined with other subway lines. These letters get recycled as new trains are created. For example, when the new 2nd Avenue train line opens, it will be called the T train. I and O were skipped because they looked too much like 1 and 0. Y and U were skipped because they sound too much like "why" and "you," and the MTA was afraid people would get confused. X is used as a placeholder by the MTA when it is planning new subway lines and so can never be a real train. That leaves only the P train. P trains have been planned in the past but have been abandoned or renamed at the last minute. There's no proof, but it's possible that the MTA simply thinks a P train would cause far too many giggles.

IRT:

1 **2** **3** **4** **5** **6** **7**

IND:

A **B** **C** **D** **E** **F** **G**

BMT:

J **L** **M** **N** **Q** **R** **S** **Z**

THE SUBWAY TODAY

Today, the New York City subway system is still digging new lines! One of the most highly anticipated projects is the completion of the 2nd Avenue line, which has been in the works since the 1920s.

Progress on the 2nd Avenue Subway as of November 23, 2013. This photo shows the future 86th Street Station.

Tunnel-boring machine in the 2nd Avenue subway, May 14, 2010.

These days, a tunnel-boring machine (TBM) does most of the difficult digging. With powerful discs and scrapers, a TBM crushes and removes rock debris in both bedrock and soft soil. It also uses many supports to safely hold up the tunnel as it moves. The only downside is that it moves very slowly, averaging a speed of thirty-five feet per day.

EMPIRE STATE BUILDING

At 1,250 feet, the Empire State Building was the world's tallest skyscraper for over forty years, until the construction of the World Trade Center in 1972. After 2001, it remained the tallest building in New York City until 2014, when One World Trade Center, which reaches 1,776 feet, was built.

Construction on the Empire State building began in 1930, and the grand opening was held on May 1, 1931. At the time, there was a speed limit for elevators: 700 feet per minute. This was too slow for such a tall skyscraper, however, so developers took a bit of a gamble and installed 1,200-foot-per-minute elevators. They expected that the Board of Standards and Appeals would amend the regulations on elevator speed, and only six months after the Empire State Building opened in 1931, it happened. The cars, which had been traveling at the lower speed, quickly sped up, creating one of the first fully functional express elevator systems in New York City! Express elevators, like express trains in the subway, skip certain stops to move thousands of people a day to the upper floors more quickly.

From "Robot Elevators to Serve 85,000 in Greatest Building" (Popular Science Monthly, 1931). Express elevators are marked in black; local elevators are marked in red.

1948 tourist postcard for the Empire State Building.

Can you follow Alicia's, Pablo's and the class's journey on the drawing above? Can you find Central Park? What other landmark skyscraper do you recognize? (Hint: look at the page on the left.)

FURTHER READING & RESOURCES.
The history of New York City and the New York City Subway System is complex and fascinating. Here's a list of books and websites you might enjoy:

THE CITY BENEATH US: BUILDING THE NEW YORK SUBWAY; New York Transit Authority with Vivian Heller. W.W. Norton, 2004. *Official history of the subway system, with photographs. Ages 10+*

SUBWAYS: THE TRACKS THAT BUILT NEW YORK CITY; Lorraine B. Diehl. Clarkson Potter, 2004. *An easy to read, informative history of the New York Subway system. Ages 12+*

THE SUBWAY AND THE CITY: CELEBRATING A CENTURY; Stan Fischler with John Henderson. Frank Merriwell, 2004. *A big book with lots of history and lots of pictures. Ages 14+*

NEW YORK UNDERGROUND: THE ANATOMY OF A CITY; Julia Solis. Routledge, 2004. *An exciting overview of the tunnels, trains, mazes and secrets underneath New York City. Ages 12+*

THE HISTORICAL ATLAS OF NEW YORK CITY: A VISUAL CELEBRATION OF 400 YEARS OF NEW YORK CITY'S HISTORY; Eric Homberger. Owl Books, 2005. *A comprehensive reference book containing maps, photos, and drawings. Ages 12+*

Online Resources:

WWW.MTA.INFO *The official website of the Metropolitan Transportation Authority, which oversees the subways, trains, and buses of New York City.*

WWW.NYCSUBWAY.ORG *A website dedicated to the history of the subway system, including photos, maps, and documents.*

Tips for Parents, Teachers, and Librarians:
TOON GRAPHICS FOR VISUAL READERS

TOON Graphics are comics and visual narratives that bring the text to life in a way that captures young readers' imaginations and makes them want to read on—and read more. When the authors are also artists, they can convey their creative vision with pictures as well as words. They can enhance the overarching theme and present important details that are absorbed by the reader along with the text. Young readers also develop their aesthetic sense when they experience the relationship of text to picture in all its communicative power.

Reading TOON Graphics is a pleasure for all. Beginners and seasoned readers alike will sharpen both their literal and inferential reading skills.

Let the pictures tell the story

The very economy of comic books necessitates the use of a reader's imaginative powers. In comics, the images often imply rather than tell outright. Readers must learn to make connections between events to complete the narrative, helping them build their ability to visualize and to make "mental maps."

A comic book also gives readers a great deal of visual context that can be used to investigate the thinking behind the characters' choices.

Pay attention to the artist's choices

Look carefully at the artwork: it offers a subtext that at first is sensed only on a subliminal level by the reader and encourages rereading. It creates a sense of continuity for the action, and it can tell you about the art, architecture, and clothing of a specific time period. It may present the atmosphere, landscape, and flora and fauna of another time or of another part of the world. TOON Graphics can also present multiple points of view and simultaneous events in a manner not permitted by linear written narration. Facial expressions and body language reveal subtle aspects of characters' personalities beyond what can be expressed by words.

Read and reread!

Readers can compare comic book artists' styles and evaluate how different authors get their point across in different ways. In investigating the author's choices, a young reader begins to gain a sense of how all literary and art forms can be used to convey the author's central ideas.

The world of TOON Graphics and of comic book art is rich and varied. Making meaning out of reading with the aid of visuals may be the best way to become a lifelong reader, one who knows how to read for pleasure and for information—a reader who *loves* to read.